Mother Goose
Picture Puzzles

Will Hillenbrand

Marshall Cavendish Children

To Margery,
a picture-perfect publisher,
editor, and friend—
no puzzle about it!

—W.H.

Text and illustrations copyright © 2011 by Will Hillenbrand

All rights reserved
Marshall Cavendish Corporation, 99 White Plains Road, Tarrytown, NY 10591
www.marshallcavendish.us/kids

Library of Congress Cataloging-in-Publication Data

Hillenbrand, Will.
Mother Goose picture puzzles / adapted and illustrated by Will Hillenbrand.
p. cm.
Summary: Nursery rhymes are presented in the form of rebuses.
ISBN 978-0-7614-5808-1
1. Nursery rhymes. 2. Children's poetry. 3. Rebuses. [1. Nursery rhymes.
2. Rebuses.] I. Title.
PZ8.3.H5542Mo 2011
398.8—dc22
[E]
2010023111

The illustrations were rendered in mixed media.
Book design by Will Hillenbrand
Editor: Margery Cuyler

Printed in China (E)
First edition
1 3 5 6 4 2

Contents

Old Mother Goose ... 5

Hey, Diddle, Diddle ... 6

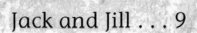

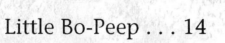

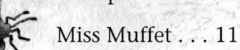
Jack and Jill ... 9

The Pumpkin-eater ... 10

Miss Muffet ... 11

Baa, Baa, Black Sheep ... 12

Little Bo-Peep ... 14

Little Boy Blue ... 17

The Black Hen ... 18

The Little Bird ... 20

Humpty Dumpty ... 22

Old King Cole ... 24

Mary, Mary, Quite Contrary ... 26

Pat-a-Cake ... 28

Polly and Sukey ... 30

Yankee Doodle ... 32

Hickory Dickory Dock ... 34

Wee Willie Winkie ... 36

There Was an Old Lady ... 38

The Star ... 40

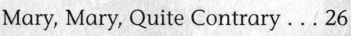

4

Old Mother Goose

Old , when

she wanted to wander,

would ride through the air

on a very fine .

Mother Goose

gander

Hey, Diddle, Diddle

Hey, diddle, diddle,

the and the ,

the jumped over the ,

the little  laughed

to see such sport,

and the 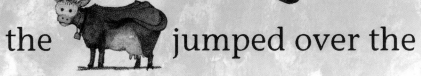 ran away with the .

cat

fiddle

6

cow

moon

spoon

dish

dog

hill

8

Jack and Jill

Jack and Jill went up the ,

to fetch a of ~~~ ;

Jack fell down, and broke his 👑,

and Jill came tumbling after.

pail

water

crown
(another word for
top of head)

The Pumpkin-eater

Peter, Peter, -eater,

had a wife and couldn't keep her;

he put her in a 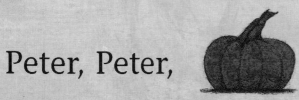 shell,

and there he kept her very 🛖.

pumpkin

Miss Muffet

Little Miss Muffet

sat on a ,

eating her ;

along came a ,

and sat down beside her,

and frightened Miss Muffet away.

well

curds and
whey

spider

tuffet

Baa, Baa, Black Sheep

Baa, baa, ,

have you any ?

Yes, sir, yes, sir.

 full;

1 for my master,

1 for my dame,

and **1** for the little boy

who lives down the lane.

black sheep

bag

wool

Little Bo-Peep

Little Bo-Peep has lost her ,

And can't tell where to find them;

Leave them alone, and they'll come ,

And bring their behind them.

tails

sheep

14

home

haystack

horn

Little Boy Blue

Little Boy Blue, come, blow your !

The 's in the meadow,

the 's in the .

Where's the little boy

that looks after the ?

Under the , fast asleep!

sheep

cow

corn

The Black Hen

Hickety, pickety, my ,

she lays for gentlemen;

gentlemen come every day

to see what my  doth lay.

black hen

18

eggs

The Little Bird

Once I saw a little

come hop, hop, hop;

so I cried, "Little ,

will you , ,  ?"

I was going to the

to say, "How do you do?"

But he shook his little 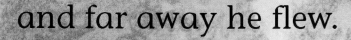,

and far away he flew.

bird

tail

STOP

window

Humpty Dumpty

Humpty Dumpty sat on a ,

Humpty Dumpty had a great fall;

all the King's ,

and all the King's

couldn't put Humpty together again.

wall

men

horses

Old King Cole

Old King Cole

was a merry old soul,

and a merry old soul was he;

he called for his 🚬 ,

and he called for his 🥣 ,

and he called for his 🎻🎻🎻 !

fiddlers three

bowl

pipe

Mary, Mary, Quite Contrary

Mary, Mary, quite contrary,

how does your garden grow?

With  and ,

and all in a row.

cockle shells

26

silver bells

pretty maids

27

Pat-a-Cake

Pat-a-cake, pat-a-cake, !

Bake me a  as fast as you can.

Pat it, and prick it, and mark it with B,

put it in the oven for  and me.

baby

28

cake

baker's man

Polly and Sukey

, put the  on,

, put the  on,

, put the  on,

and let's drink .

Polly

kettle

, take it off again,

, take it off again,

, take it off again,

they've all gone away.

Sukey

tea

Yankee Doodle

Yankee Doodle went to town,

riding on a  ;

he stuck a in his ,

and called it macaroni.

feather

hat

pony

33

Hickory Dickory Dock

Hickory, dickory, dock,

the  ran up the .

The clock struck 1,

the ran down,

hickory, dickory, dock.

mouse

clock

one

Wee Willie Winkie

 runs

through the town,

upstairs and downstairs,

in his nightgown;

rapping at the 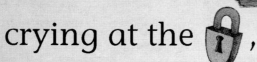 ,

crying at the  ,

"Are the children in their beds?

Now it's **8** o'clock."

There Was an Old Lady

There was an old lady who lived in a .

She had so many children

she didn't know what to do.

She gave them some

without any .

She hugged them and kissed them

and put them to .

broth

bread

bed

shoe

The Star

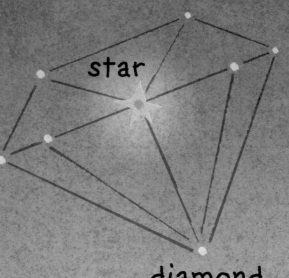

star

diamond

Twinkle, twinkle, little ⭐,

how I wonder what you are!

Up above the world so high,

like a 💍 in the sky.

Twinkle, twinkle, little ⭐,

how I wonder what you are!